INTO the WOODS

STEPHEN SONDHEIM
JAMES LAPINE

INTO the WOODS

ADAPTED AND ILLUSTRATED
BY HUDSON TALBOTT

CROWN PUBLISHERS, INC.
NEW YORK

PART I

ONCE UPON A TIME,

in a far-off kingdom, there lived . . .

a fair young maiden, a sad young lad,

and a childless baker with his wife.

The maiden, called Cinderella, wished more than anything, more than life, to go to the King's festival.

The lad, named Jack, also had a wish. He wished, more than anything, more than life, more than riches, that his cow would give him some milk.

The Baker and the Baker's Wife were wishing, too. They wished more than anything, more than life, more than riches, more than the moon, that they had a child.

Cinderella's mother had died, and her father had taken for his new wife a woman with two daughters of her own. All three were beautiful of face but vile and black of heart. And, jealous of Cinderella's good qualities, they cruelly thrust upon her the dirtiest tasks around the house.

"*You* wish to go to the festival?" the Stepmother asked mockingly.

"Look at your nails!" chuckled Lucinda, one of Cinderella's stepsisters.

"Look at your dress!" giggled Florinda, the other.

"You wish to go to the festival and dance before the Prince?!" they all exclaimed, and fell down laughing out of control.

Jack, on the other hand, had no father. And his mother was concerned about her son and his devotion to his cow, Milky-White.

"You foolish child! What in Heaven's name are you doing with the cow *inside* the house?" she demanded.

"A warm environment might be just what Milky-White needs to produce his milk," replied Jack.

"It's a *she*! How many times must I tell you? Only *shes* can give milk! Besides, she's been dry for a week straight. We've no food or money and no choice but to sell her while she can still command a price."

"But Milky-White is my best friend in the whole world," Jack pleaded.

"Look at her! There are bugs on her dugs. There are flies in her eyes. There's a lump on her rump big enough to be a hump. We've no time to sit and dither while her withers wither with her. And no one keeps a cow for a friend!"

6

That same afternoon, as the Baker and his wife were preparing the next day's bread, a little girl with a big appetite and a lovely red cape called. She wished to bring a loaf of bread to her poor old Grandmother, who lived in the woods. As the Baker wrapped a loaf, the child eyed the fresh pastries. With the bread tucked into her basket, Little Red Ridinghood started off for the woods, also managing to take three small pies, two sticky buns, two cream puffs, and a layer cake with her.

"Into the woods, it's time to go. I hate to leave. I have to, though. Into the woods to Grandmother's house, I must begin the journey."

"You're certain of your way?" asked the Baker's Wife.

"Into the woods and down the dell. The path is straight, I know it well. Into the woods to bring some bread to Granny, who is sick in bed. Never can tell what lies ahead. For all that I know, she's already dead. But into the woods, then out of the woods, and home before dark!"

Meanwhile, the Stepmother was playing a cruel joke on Cinderella.

"I have emptied a pot of lentils into the ashes," she told the girl. "If you have picked them out again in two hours' time, you shall go to the festival with us."

But the Stepmother was unaware that Cinderella had friends in high places. No sooner had the cruel woman left than Cinderella sang out:

> *"Birds in the sky,*
> *Birds in the eaves,*
> *In the leaves,*
> *In the fields,*
> *In the castles and ponds.*
> *Quick, little birds,*
> *Flick through the ashes.*
> *Pick and peck and sift,*
> *But swiftly.*
> *Put the lentils into my pot."*

As she sang, flocks of birds fluttered down into the ashes and busily set to work sorting out the lentils and dropping them into the pot. The task completed, Cinderella thanked them, bade them farewell, and awaited the Stepmother's return.

Because the Baker had lost his mother and father in a baking accident—or so he believed—he was eager to have a family of his own and was concerned that all efforts had failed. The reason for this misfortune was explained to him that afternoon when the creepy old Witch from next door paid them a visit.

"What do you wish?" the Baker asked.

"It's not what I wish. It's what *you* wish," the hag cackled as she pointed to his wife's belly. "Nothing cooking in there now, is there?"

The ancient enchantress went on to tell the couple that she had placed a spell on their house. "In the past," she informed the Baker, "when you were no more than a baby, your father brought your mother and you to this cottage. She was with child, and she developed an unusual appetite. She took one look at my beautiful garden and told your father that what she wanted more than anything in the world was greens, greens, and nothing but greens! Parsley, peppers, cabbages and celery, asparagus and watercress and fiddleferns and lettuce!

"He said, 'All right,' but it wasn't, quite, 'cause I caught him in the autumn in my garden one night! He was robbing me, raping me, rooting through my rutabaga, raiding my arugula, and ripping up the rampion. My champion! My favorite! I should have laid a spell on him right there. Could have turned him into stone or a dog or a chair. . ."

At which point, the Witch went into a trance, shuddering and gurgling with ghastly noises of joy. The Baker and the Wife could only stand by, trembling with fear, when without warning the Witch continued chattily.

"But I let him have the rampion—I'd lots to spare. In return, however, I said, 'Fair is fair: You can let me have the baby that your wife will bear. And we'll call it square.'"

"I had a brother?" asked the Baker.

"No. . .but you had a sister," the Witch hissed. However, she refused to tell him any more of his sister—not even that her name was Rapunzel.

"I thought I had been more than reasonable," the Witch continued petulantly, "and we all might have lived happily thereafter. But how was I to know what he'd also put in his pocket?! You see, when I had inherited that garden, my mother warned me that I would be punished if ever I were to lose any of the beans."

"Beans?" asked the couple.

"The special beans! I let him go, I didn't know he'd stolen my beans! I was watching him crawl back over the wall when *bang! crash!* and the lightning flash! and the —never mind, that's another story.

"Anyway, at last the big day came, and I made my claim. 'Oh, don't take away the baby,' they shrieked and screeched, but I did, and I hid her where she'll never be reached! And your father cried and your mother died when, for extra measure (I admit it was a pleasure), I said, 'Sorry, I'm still not mollified.' And I laid a little spell on them— you too, son—that your family tree would always be a barren one . . ."

She chuckled with glee, the chuckle rising to a chortle, the chortle to a cackle, the cackle to a scream, the very stool she sat on rising into the air along with her excitement.

"Sooooo," she continued, coming back to earth along with the stool, "there's no more fuss, and there's no more scenes, and my garden thrives—you should see my nectarines—but I'm telling you the same I tell kings and queens: Don't ever never ever mess around with my greens! Especially the beans!"

Turning to observe the effect of her story, the Witch found her listeners paralyzed and thoroughly intimidated. Nevertheless, she had not come on this particular afternoon to needle but to negotiate.

"You wish to have the curse reversed?" she said after a rather pregnant pause, so to speak. "I'll need a certain potion first. Go to the wood and bring me back:

One, the cow as white as milk.
Two, the cape as red as blood.
Three, the hair as yellow as corn.
Four, the slipper as pure as gold.

Bring me these before the chime of midnight in three days' time, and you shall have, I guarantee, a child as perfect as child can be. Go to the wood!"

With that, she disappeared in a smelly puff of smoke.

At Jack's house, his mother was beginning to despair.

"Now listen to me, Jack. Lead Milky-White to market and fetch the best price you can. Take no less than five pounds," she said.

"No more than five pounds," Jack replied.

"*Less!* Less than five," his mother repeated, pinching his ear hard. "Into the woods with you, to market, to sell the cow."

"Into the woods to sell a friend," sighed Jack as he reluctantly led Milky-White out of the house.

"Some day you'll have a real pet, Jack," his mother called by way of encouragement.

"A piggy?" he shouted back.

Jack's Mother didn't reply but just shook her head sadly as she closed the door.

Meanwhile, as her family was preparing to leave for the festival, Cinderella rushed forward with the pot of lentils, pleading, "Now may I go to the festival?"

"The festival?!" The Stepmother was aghast to see that the lentils had been collected. "Darling, those nails! Darling, those clothes! Lentils are one thing but, darling, with those you'd make us the fools of the festival and mortify the Prince!"

"The carriage is waiting," Cinderella's father declared, entering the room.

With a flourish, the family left the house. "Good night, Father," Cinderella cried out sadly. But he ignored her as had become his way, leaving Cinderella alone.

As the Baker dressed for his quest in the woods, he discovered something in his pocket.

"Look what I found in Father's hunting jacket," he said to his wife. "Six beans. I wonder if they are the Witch's—"

"Special beans?" asked the Wife. "We'll take them with us."

"No," said the Baker, "you are not coming. The spell is on my house. Only I can lift the spell."

"No, no," countered the Wife. "The spell is on *our* house. We must lift the spell together."

"No," said the Baker again, "you are not to come, and that is final. Now what is it that I'm to find?"

"You don't remember?!" she exclaimed.

"The cow as white as milk.
The cape as red as blood.
The hair as yellow as corn.
The slipper as pure as gold."
Repeating the list to himself,
the Baker set out alone
for the woods.

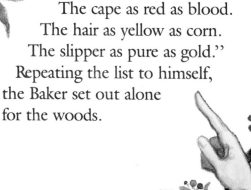

Meanwhile, Cinderella sat dejected, tearfully pondering her situation. "I still wish to go to the festival, but how am I ever to get to the festival? I know!" she cried. "I'll visit Mother's grave and tell her I wish to go to the festival!"

So into the enchanted forest they went: Cinderella to visit her mother's grave; the Baker to fetch the ingredients for the Witch's potion; Jack to sell his cow; and Little Red Ridinghood to bring her Grandmother a loaf of bread.

Their mission was simple: Into the woods without delay, but careful not to lose the way. Into the woods, who knows what may be lurking on the journey? Into the woods to get the thing that makes it worth the journeying.

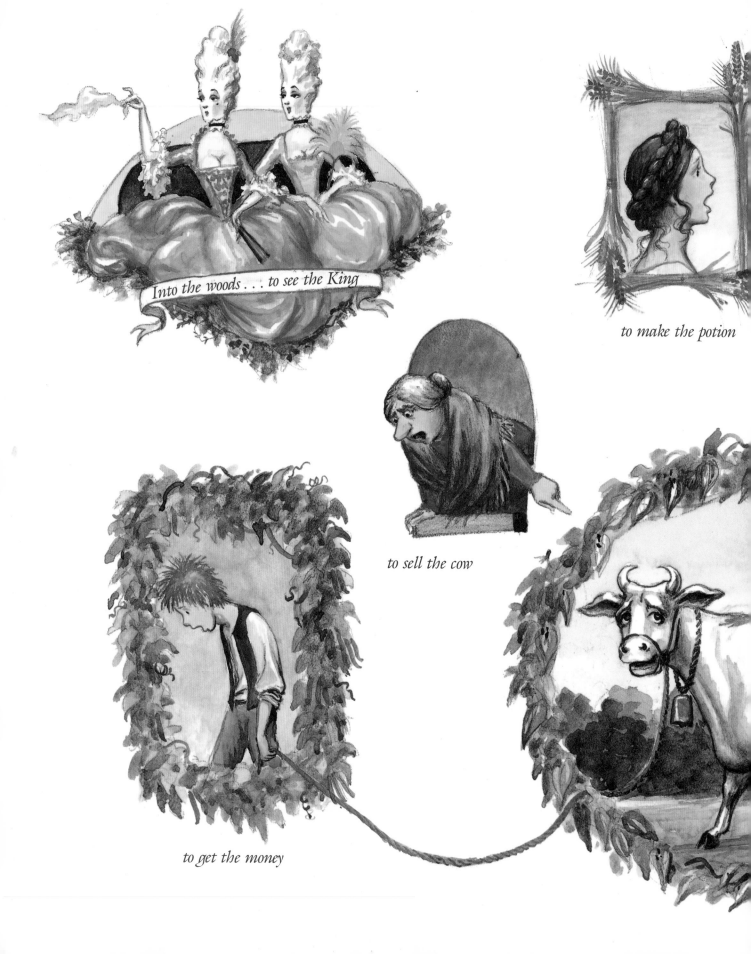

Into the woods . . . to see the King

to make the potion

to sell the cow

to get the money

to lift the spell

to go to the festival

to Grandmother's house

Into the woods,
then out of the woods,
and home before dark!

CINDERELLA HAD PLANTED a branch at the grave of her mother, and she visited it so often, and wept so much, that her tears had watered it until it had become a handsome tree.

"I've been good and I've been kind, Mother," she whimpered, kneeling at the base of the tree, "doing only what I learned from you. Why then am I left behind, Mother? Is there something more that I should do? What is wrong with me, Mother? Something must be wrong. I wish—"

Suddenly a gentle breeze rustled the leaves, and her mother's ghost appeared in the branches.

"Quit whining, dear, and pull yourself together," said the ghost. "Opportunity is not a lengthy visitor, and good fortune, like bad, can befall when least expected. Do you know what you wish? Are you certain what you wish is what you want? If you know what you want, then make a wish. Ask the tree and you shall have your wish."

Cinderella hesitated a moment and then, looking up into the branches at the wonderful, shimmering maze, she whispered, "Shiver and quiver, little tree. Silver and gold throw down on me."

A stronger breeze stirred the foliage as the sunlight was gradually replaced by moonlight. Like thread, the rays of light began to dance and spin until a gown as sheer and fine as the lace of damselfly wings emerged, followed by a pair of jewellike golden slippers. They floated downward, ever so softly, and before she could draw another breath, Cinderella was dressed and on her way to the festival.

Elsewhere in the woods, Jack was leading Milky-White to market. He stopped to rest and was startled to hear his own name called.

"Hello, Jack."

He turned around just in time to see a peculiar Old Man step out from behind a tree.

"How did you know my name?" Jack asked.

"When first I appear, I seem mysterious. But when explained, I am nothing serious."

"Say that again," requested Jack.

But instead the Old Man asked him how much he wanted for Milky-White.

"No less than five pounds," replied the boy, carefully remembering.

"Why, you'd be lucky to exchange her for a sack of beans," the Old Man scoffed, but before Jack could ask what he meant, the Old Man disappeared as quickly as he had arrived.

At the same time, in another part of the woods, Little Red Ridinghood was skipping along on her way to Granny's. She hadn't gone far when she was greeted by a tall, dark, and hairy character.

"Good day, young lady."

"Good day, Mr. Wolf," she replied, skipping onward.

"Whither away so hurriedly?" inquired the Wolf, licking his chops.

"To my Grandmother's."

"And where might your Grandmother live?"

"A good quarter of a league farther into the woods," answered the little girl. "Her house stands under three large oak trees."

The Wolf grunted lasciviously and thought to himself as he watched her skip away, "Look at that flesh, pink and plump. Tender and fresh, not one lump."

The Wolf smacked his lips, then ran over and popped up in front of her again. "Hello, little girl, what's your rush?" he asked coyly. "You're missing all the flowers. The sun won't set for hours. Take your time."

But the little girl wasn't easily deterred. "Mother said, 'Straight ahead, not to delay or be misled,' " she replied curtly. " 'Come what may, follow the path and never stray.' "

"Just so, little girl," cooed the Wolf. "Any path! So many worth exploring. Just one can be so boring, and look what you're ignoring," he added, gesturing toward the patches of wildflowers.

As Little Red Ridinghood paused and stooped to gather a bouquet, the Wolf, now almost beside himself quivering with excitement, fantasized about the day's possibilities: "Grandmother first, then Miss Plump. What a delectable couple! Utter perfection: one brittle, one supple. Think of those crisp, aging bones, then something fresh on the palate. Think of that scrumptious carnality twice in one day. There's no possible way to describe what you feel when you're talking to your meal. . . ."

Eager to get to Grandmother's house, the Wolf bid a polite farewell to the girl, who was now wandering deeper into the woods to collect more flowers. "Good-bye, little girl," he said, salivating, adding

under his breath, "and hello." And he loped off rapidly to Grand-mother's house.

The Baker, unbeknownst, had witnessed their exchange.

"Is harm to come to that little girl in the red cape?" he asked himself.

"Forget the girl and get the cape!" screeched a familiar voice from behind him: that of the Witch, descending from a nearby tree.

"You frightened me," gasped the Baker.

"That's the cape!" the Witch said. "Get it! Get it!"

"How am I supposed to get it?"

"You go up to the little thing, and you take it!" she shrieked impatiently.

"I can't just take a cloak from a little girl. Why don't *you* take it?" asked the Baker.

"If I could, I would!" she screamed. "Get me what I need! Get me what I need!" And the Witch vanished into the foliage.

"This is ridiculous," the Baker thought. "I'll never get that red cape or find a golden cow, or a yellow slipper—or was it a golden slipper and a yellow cow? Oh, no . . ."

"The cow as white as milk, the hair as yellow as corn, the slipper as pure as gold," sounded another familiar voice.

The Baker turned to find his wife. "What are you doing?" he asked angrily. "You have no business being alone here, and you have no idea what I have come upon. You would be frightened for your life. Now go home immediately."

"I wish to help," protested the Wife.

"The spell is on my house," said the Baker. "Only I can lift the spell."

"The spell is on *our* house," she argued. "We must lift the spell together." They continued to bicker until the nearby sound of cloven hooves interrupted them. It was Milky-White, led by Jack. The Wife's eyes widened at the sight of the cow. She whispered to her husband as she nudged him forward, "A cow as white as—"

"Milk," he finished, and nervously put forth a greeting. "Hello, young man."

"Hello, sir," said Jack.

"What might you be doing in the middle of the forest with a cow?" asked the Baker.

"I was heading toward market, but I seem to have lost my way," Jack answered.

"And what were you planning to do there?" asked the Baker, eyeing the cow.

"Sell my cow, sir. No less than five pounds."

The Baker turned to his wife. "Five pounds, where am I to get five pounds?" he whispered anxiously.

The Wife turned to Jack and said, "She must be generous of milk to fetch five pounds."

"Yes, ma'am," Jack replied hesitantly. Innocence rendered him a poor liar.

"And if you can't fetch that sum? Then what are you to do?" continued the Wife.

"I suppose my mother and I will have no food to eat," murmured Jack, scratching his head.

The Baker, meanwhile, had searched his pockets to find only the six beans. His wife looked at them and said loudly, for Jack's benefit, "Beans, we mustn't give up our beans. . . . Well, if you feel we must. . . . Beans will bring you food, son."

"Beans in exchange for my cow?" challenged Jack.

"Oh, these are no ordinary beans. These beans carry magic."

"Magic? What kind of magic?"

The Wife, dragging her husband into the deception, pushed him toward the boy. "Tell him."

"Magic that defies description," he hesitantly replied.

"How many beans?" asked Jack, thinking of what the Mysterious Old Man had said.

"Six," said the Baker.

"Five," interposed the Wife hastily. "We can't part with all of them. Besides, I'd say they're worth a pound each, at the very least."

"Could I buy my cow back someday?"

"Well, possibly," said the Baker uncomfortably, handing Jack the five beans.

Jack turned to Milky-White, who was only beginning to grasp the full scope of the situation. "I guess this is good-bye, old pal," he said haltingly. "You've been a perfect friend. Someday I'll buy you back. I'll see you soon again. I hope that when I do, it won't be on a plate."

With a last tearful kiss on her large, wet nose, Jack bid adieu to Milky-White and fled the scene, overcome with grief.

The Baker handed Milky-White's lead to his wife and sternly ordered her to take the cow and go home. He was angry. "Magic beans!" he said with disgust. "We've no reason to believe they're magic. Are we going to dispel this curse through deceit?"

"No one would have given him more for that creature," said the Wife. "We did him a favor. At least they'll have some food."

"Five beans!" shouted the Baker.

"If you know what you want, then you go and you find it and you get it," lectured the Wife.

The Baker pointed in the direction of their home.

"Do we want a child or not?" she insisted. "There are rights and wrongs and in-betweens, no one waits when fortune intervenes. And maybe they're really magic. Who knows? When the end's in sight you'll realize that if the end is right, it justifies the beans!"

Once again the Baker ordered his wife home, saying that he would carry things out in his own fashion, and they parted.

Unfortunately, Jack's Mother was not as easy to convince of the beans' value. Her son returned home, only to have her angrily throw the beans out of the window and send him to bed without his supper.

DEEP IN THE FOREST there stood a doorless tower, and in this tower lived a beautiful young maiden with the most magnificent mane of golden hair, which she always combed. Her name was Rapunzel, and she was the child taken by the Witch from the Baker's mother and father. The Witch, careful not to lose this beauty to the outside world, kept her shut within the tower, and when she wanted to visit she placed herself beneath it and cried, "Rapunzel, Rapunzel, let down your hair to me."

By chance one day, a Prince happened upon this very scene. He had followed the haunting sound of Rapunzel's voice as she sang a wordless song to herself, something she often did to pass the time. "Rapunzel, Rapunzel. What a strange name," the Prince said to himself. "Strange, but beautiful. Tomorrow, before that horrible witch arrives, I will stand beneath her window and ask her to let down her hair to *me*."

"Not so fast, young man," said a voice. "What makes you think you can have her?" The Mysterious Old Man peered through the underbrush at the Prince.

"Who are you?" asked the Prince.

"When first I appear, I seem imperious, but when explained, I am nothing serious."

"Don't speak in riddles, old man. I am a prince."

"And how will you get her from that tower? What makes you think your princely position can save you from the Witch's powers?"

"Go away, old man," the royal youth replied arrogantly, and he turned again to the tower.

"You have been warned," said the Old Man, "and you shall not see your future." And with that, he disappeared into the brush, leaving the Prince to ponder how in fact he would get Rapunzel from her tower.

The Baker was pondering, too. How was he to get Little Red Ridinghood's cape? Perhaps the method of bartering that had worked so well with Jack in obtaining the cow would work again? When he finally caught up to her, he cleared his throat and feebly attempted conversation. "Hello there, little one. I hope you've saved some of those sweets for Granny," he said, having noticed the dark ring of chocolate around her mouth. "Where did you get that cape? I so admire it."

"My Granny made it for me," replied the child.

"Is that right?" said the Baker. "I would love a red cloak like that."

"You'd look pretty silly," she said, giggling.

Sensing his moment, the Baker nimbly slipped the cape from the child's shoulders and asked politely for a closer look.

"I don't like to be without my cape," fretted the child. "Please give it back."

"An exchange for it," proposed the Baker. "I'll give you some money or a magic bean—or all the sweets you can eat—and you can tell your Granny you lost it and she'll make you another."

"Give it back, please,"
repeated the child, urgently this time.

"I want it badly," whined the Baker. The Witch's haunting words rumbled through his head: "You go up to the little thing and you take it. Take it, take it, *take it!*" Impulsively, he sprang away into the forest with the cape gripped tightly in hand.

The child stood numbly for a moment, in shock. Then she began to tremble more and more violently until her lungs burst forth with a bloodcurdling scream that echoed through the forest. Trees shook and wildlife scattered as the child exploded into hysterics. Within a moment the Baker was standing before her again, looking shamefaced and returning the cloak.

"I just wanted to make sure you really loved this cape," he said lamely. "Now go to your Granny's and be careful that no wolf comes your way."

"I'd rather a wolf than you, any day," huffed the little girl, and with that she ran off, stamping on his toe for good measure.

"I should have kept it," winced the Baker, annoyed with himself. "What's more important: that she have that silly cloak or that I have a child of my own?" And so, with newfound determination, he followed in pursuit of the cape.

As for Little Red Ridinghood, she was surprised to find her Grandmother's cottage door standing open. "Oh, dear, how uneasy I feel," said the child to herself. "Perhaps it's all the sweets that I've eaten."

But, in fact, the child's uneasiness was well founded, for just prior to her arrival the Wolf had come, devoured Granny, donned her nightcap and gown, and crawled into her bed. He now lay waiting for his next course.

"Good day, Grandmother," said the girl as she cautiously entered the cottage. "My, you're looking very strange. What big ears you have."

"The better to hear you with, my dear," said the Wolf, trying to sound like an old woman.

"But, Grandmother, what big eyes you have," observed the girl.

"The better to see you with, my dear," said the Wolf.

"But, Grandmother, what large hands you have."

"The better to hug you with, my dear," said the Wolf.

"Oh, Grandmother, what a terrible big wet mouth you have!"

"The better to eat you with!" Scarcely had the Wolf said this than with a single bound he was devouring the little girl.

Well, it had been a full day of eating for both of them. His appetite appeased, the Wolf took to bed for a nice, long nap. As he slept, the Baker arrived at the cottage.

"*Zzzzzzzzzzzzzz!!!*"

Puzzled by the ungrandmotherly snore, the Baker entered and followed the sounds to the bedroom. "Grandmother, ha!" he exclaimed, discovering the Wolf asleep. As he drew a knife from the sheath on his belt, he noticed a bit of red cloth in the corner of the Wolf's mouth. He knew then that he must get the cape from within the Wolf's stomach. He took the knife and slit the Wolf's belly open to find not only the cape, but Little Red Ridinghood and Granny—intact!

"What a fright," said the child, stepping out of the open stomach. "How dark it was inside that wolf!"

"Let's see the demon sliced into a thousand bits," wheezed Granny as she emerged from the inner regions. "Better yet, take the knife and cut his evil head off!"

"Well, I'll leave you to your task," said the Baker queasily, trying to exit.

"Don't you want the skins?" Granny inquired. "What kind of a hunter are you?"

"I'm a baker!" he protested.

Little Red Ridinghood, knowing what the Baker really wanted, untied her cape and placed it in his hands. "Here, Mr. Baker. You saved our lives."

"Are you certain?" asked the Baker, astonished.

"Yes," replied the girl. "Maybe Granny will make me another with the skins of this wolf."

And so, with the second item in hand, feeling braver and more confident than he had ever felt, the Baker returned to the woods.

IN THE MEANTIME, the Baker's Wife was dutifully on her way home with Milky-White in tow, when who should stumble and fall across her path but Cinderella in full ball regalia.

"Are you all right?" asked the Wife, helping the young woman up from the ground.

"Yes," gasped Cinderella. "I just need to catch my breath."

"What a beautiful gown you're wearing. Were you at the King's festival?" continued the Wife. "And why are you in the woods at this hour?"

Cinderella was about to answer, but the sound of approaching voices caught her ear. In a sudden panic, she motioned to the Baker's Wife to keep quiet and ducked behind the seated cow.

With a flourish of trumpets, the Prince and his Steward appeared. "Have you seen a beautiful young woman in a ball gown pass through?" the Prince demanded of the Baker's Wife.

"I don't think so, sir," she replied hesitantly.

"I think I see her over there," called the Steward, looking into the distance and dashing off. The Prince glanced back at the Wife and then followed.

"I've never lied to royalty before," murmured the Wife to herself. "I've never *anything* to royalty before."

"Thank you," said Cinderella, stepping out from behind Milky-White.

"If a prince were looking for me, I certainly wouldn't hide," observed the Wife.

"What brings you here?" asked Cinderella in an effort to change the subject. "And with a cow?"

"Oh, my husband is somewhere in the woods. He's undoing a spell," she stated proudly. "Now, the Prince. What was he like?"

Cinderella sighed. "He's a very nice prince."

"And . . . ?" probed the Wife, still enthralled by her encounter with the dashing Prince.

"And it was a very nice ball."

"And . . . the Prince . . . ?"

"Oh, yes, the Prince. . . . Well, he's tall."

"Is that all? Did you dance? Is he charming? They say that he's charming."

"We did nothing *but* dance," replied Cinderella wearily. "Still, it made a nice change."

"But the Prince . . . !"

Cinderella shrugged. "He has charm, for a prince, I guess. I don't meet a wide range." She paused, growing thoughtful. "And it's all very strange."

"Are you to return to the festival tomorrow?" asked the Wife. "I understand it's to be a three-day festival."

"Perhaps," said the girl.

"Perhaps? Oh, to be pursued by a prince. All that pursues me is tomorrow's bread. What I wouldn't give to be in your shoes," declared the Wife, her eyes drifting downward. Suddenly, she caught sight of Cinderella's shoes: slippers as pure as gold.

Just then, Cinderella noticed in the distance a giant vine growing next to a small cottage—the cottage where Jack and his mother lived—and pointed it out to the Baker's Wife.

The Wife, however, paid no attention. She was distracted by Cinderella's footwear. Suddenly, Cinderella, hearing the chimes of midnight, exclaimed, "I must be off," and rushed into the woods. The Wife began to follow the young girl until she noticed Milky-White galloping away in the opposite direction and, after a moment's deliberation, she ran back to catch the cow.

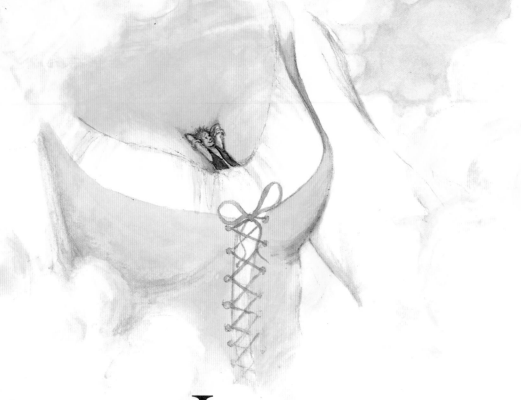

I T SO HAPPENED that the beans for which Jack had traded Milky-White were indeed magic and had sprung up overnight, intertwining themselves into an enormous beanstalk that stretched into the heavens. Unbeknownst to his mother, Jack climbed it and discovered a land of giants at the top. While exploring it, he came upon an enormously wealthy couple (that is to say, both enormous and wealthy). With her husband away, the Giantess befriended the lad and gave him warmth and protection. When the Giant came home, Jack fled in terror, snatching what he could of the Giant's fortune of gold, and scrambled down the beanstalk.

After turning most of the booty over to his mother, he bounded out the door to find and reclaim Milky-White. He was in luck, for he soon came upon the slumbering Baker huddled by a tree after an exhausting night in the woods.

Reaching into his pocket, Jack boasted, "Good fortune! Good fortune, sir! Look what I have—here are five gold pieces."

The Baker examined the coins as Jack asked, "Where is Milky-White?"

"She's back home with my wife," replied the Baker.

"Let's go find them," said Jack, starting out for the Baker's cottage.

"Wait!" the Baker protested. "I don't know that I wish to sell."

"But you said that I might buy her back," objected Jack.

"I know, but I'm not certain five gold pieces would—"

"Are you saying you wish more money?"

"More money is always—"

"Keep this," said Jack, handing him the money. "I will go fetch more." And without waiting for a reply, the boy ran off.

The Baker thought aloud, "With this money I could buy baking supplies for a year. I could buy a new slate roof and a new chimney."

"But could you buy yourself a child?" interrupted a voice from the underbrush. Slowly the Mysterious Old Man rose to reveal himself.

"Who are you?" asked the Baker.

"When first I appear, I seem delirious. But when explained, I am nothing serious," said the Old Man. With these words his tone changed. "How badly do you wish a child? Five gold pieces? Ten? Twenty?"

"I've not thought to put a price on such things," mumbled the Baker sheepishly.

"Exactly. You've not thought of many things, have you, son?" observed the Old Man, snatching the gold from the Baker's hand.

"Give it back!" shouted the Baker. "It's not your money!"

"Nor is it Jack's. The money is not what's important. What's important is that your wish be honored." And so saying, the Mysterious Old Man stepped round a tree and disappeared. The Baker darted about looking for him, but to no avail. What he did find, however, was his wife walking down the trail.

"What are you doing here?" he demanded.

She cleared her throat and smiled with determination. "I see you have the cape."

"Yes," said her husband, "only two items left to locate."

"Three," said the Wife in a weak voice.

"Two," insisted the Baker. "I've the cape and the cow."

"You've the cape!" she said tearfully.

"What have you done with the cow?"

"She ran away. I've been looking for her all night."

"I should have known better than to entrust her to you."

"She might just as easily have run from you!"

"But she didn't!"

As usual, they began to bicker, till suddenly the Witch flew in.

"Who cares?" the Witch screamed. *"The cow is gone! Get it back! Get it back!"*

"We were just going to do that," said the Baker fearfully, holding out the cape to appease her. "I can give you this—"

"Don't give me that!" the Witch shrieked. "I don't want to touch that! Fool! By tomorrow's midnight deliver the four items, or you will wish you never thought to have a child." And she vanished as quickly as she had appeared.

"I don't like that woman," said the Baker.

"I'm sorry I lost the cow," the Wife said contritely.

"I'm sorry I yelled. Now, please go back to the village."

Dejected, the Wife began to retreat.

"I will make things right," the Baker offered, "and then we can just go about our life. No more hunting about in the woods for strange objects. No more witches and dim-witted boys and hungry little girls. . . ."

But as the Baker's Wife was making her way home, she chanced to stumble upon the two princes. Curious about royalty but not wanting to be noticed, she hid in the bushes and listened to their conversation.

"There you are, good brother," she overheard Rapunzel's Prince saying to Cinderella's. "Father and I had wondered where you had gone."

"I've been looking all night for the beautiful one with whom I danced all evening" was the reply.

"Where did she go?"

"Disappeared, like the fine morning mist."

"She was lovely?"

"The loveliest."

"I'm not certain of that. I must confess that I too have found a lovely maiden. She lives here in the forest."

"The forest?" inquired Cinderella's Prince.

"Yes. In the top of a tall tower that has no door or stairs," asserted the other.

"And how do you manage a visit?"

"I stand beneath her tower and say, 'Rapunzel, Rapunzel, let down your hair to me.' And then she lowers the longest, most beautiful head of hair—yellow as corn—which I climb to her."

The Baker's Wife could hardly contain her glee at hearing the description of Rapunzel's hair, the third of the Witch's items.

"Where is this tower?" Cinderella's Prince queried.

"Two leagues due east, just beyond the mossy knoll," replied his brother.

"Rapunzel? *Rapunzel?* What kind of name is that? You jest. I've never heard of such a thing."

"I speak the truth. She is as true as your maiden. A maiden running from a prince? None would run from us."

"Yet one has," mused Cinderella's Prince wistfully. "Did I abuse her or show her disdain? Why does she run from me? Agony, beyond power of speech! When the one thing you want is the only thing out of your reach."

But Rapunzel's Prince was lost in his own problems. "High in her tower, she sits by the hour, maintaining her hair. Blithe and becoming and frequently humming a lighthearted air. . . . Agony, far more painful than yours! When I know she would go with me, if there only were doors. . . ."

"Am I not sensitive, clever, well-mannered, considerate, passionate, charming, as kind as I'm handsome, and heir to the throne?" asked his brother.

"You are everything maidens could wish for," avowed the other.

"The girl must be mad!"

"You know nothing of madness," Rapunzel's Prince reflected, "till you're climbing her hair and you see her up there, and you're nearing her, all the while hearing her. . . ."

"Always ten steps behind . . ."

"Always ten feet below . . ."

"Agony!" they agreed.

After indulging the self-pity that often plagues lovelorn princes, they resolved to marry their respective maidens and departed together through the forest.

"Two princes!" sighed the Baker's Wife, emerging from her hiding place. "Each more handsome than the other." She began to drift after them but abruptly caught herself. "No, get the hair," she said, and marched off toward Rapunzel's tower.

Elsewhere, the Baker was searching for the cow when the Mysterious Old Man, this time with Milky-White in tow, surprised him again. Before the Baker could ask him where he had found the cow, the Old Man disappeared. Not one to look a gift cow in the mouth, the Baker shrugged off this unexpected development and quickly led the cow away.

"*What are you doing?*" snarled the Witch, popping up behind the Old Man and startling him.

"I am here to make amends," said the Old Man, collecting himself.

"I want you to stay out of this," hissed the Witch.

"I am here to see that your wish is granted."

"You've caused enough trouble, old man. Keep out of my path," the Witch warned, flinging fire at his feet. The Old Man scampered off in one direction, the Witch in another.

THE BAKER'S WIFE, having traveled the two leagues east, arrived at Rapunzel's tower.

"Rapunzel, Rapunzel, let down your hair to me," she called nervously, imitating the Prince's voice. And as the golden hair billowed down from the window, the Baker's Wife reached up and selected a few strands.

"Excuse me for this," the Wife muttered as she strenuously tugged at them. With a final yank and a yelp from above, she liberated the strands from Rapunzel's benighted scalp.

Apologetic but happy, the Wife hastily departed. She had gone only a short distance, however, when Cinderella, fleeing from the second night's ball, came tumbling across her path again.

"You do take plenty of spills, don't you?" clucked the Baker's Wife as she helped the girl from the ground and brushed her off once more.

Cinderella looked up and recognized her friend from the night before. "It's these slippers," she complained as she sat down on a tree stump and took one off. "They're not suited for these surroundings. Actually, they're not much suited for dancing, either."

The Baker's Wife quietly sat down beside her, transfixed by the troublesome shoes. "I'd say those slippers were as pure as gold," she said.

"Yes," replied Cinderella. "They are all I could wish for in beauty."

Changing her tack, the Wife asked, "Was the ball just as wonderful as last evening's?"

"Yes, but I have no experience with princes and castles and gowns."

At the distant sound of blaring trumpets and men's voices, Cinderella looked around and stood up. "I must run," she whispered, slipping a shoe back on.

The Wife lunged for the remaining slipper. "And I need your shoe," she insisted, struggling to wrest it from Cinderella's grasp.

"Stop that!" cried Cinderella, grabbing back the slipper and running away just before the Prince's arrival.

"Where did she go?" the Prince demanded breathlessly.

The Wife pointed to where Cinderella had fled. "She went in that direction. I was trying to hold her here for you."

"I can capture my own damsel, thank you," snapped the Prince as he dashed off in pursuit.

The Wife watched the Prince and his retinue disappear into the woods. As she turned back, she discovered her husband standing nearby with Milky-White. He was disgruntled that he had found no more items and that his wife had still not returned home. "I've had no luck," he said.

"You've the cow!" she said excitedly.

"Yes. I've only two of the four."

"Three!" she replied, pulling out the golden threads of Rapunzel's hair. She told him of the maiden in the tower and how she had come close to capturing the golden slipper as well.

With this news, the Baker's face brightened. "We've an entire day left. Surely we can locate the slipper by then," he piped, his optimism restored.

" 'We'?" she asked incredulously. "You mean you'll allow me to stay?"

"Well," he answered with reluctance, "perhaps it will take the two of us to get this child."

"You've changed," observed the Wife. "You're daring; you're different in the woods. More sure, more sharing. You're getting us through the woods."

"It takes two," replied the Baker. "I thought one was enough—it's not true. You came through when the journey was rough. It took you. It took two of us."

"We've changed, we're strangers—I'm meeting you in the woods," she said. "Who minds what dangers? I know we'll get past the woods."

"And when we're past, let's hope the changes last," they agreed in unison, "beyond woods, beyond witches and slippers and hoods, beyond lies. It takes trust. It takes just a bit more and we're done. We want four, we had none, we've got three. We need one. It takes two."

But this moment of marital harmony was soon interrupted as another disturbance hurtled toward them from the dark. Squawking at the top of her lungs and with feathers fully ruffled, an enormous red hen broke through the underbrush. Jack was hot on her trail.

"Stop her!" he yelled. "Stop that hen!"

As the hen scurried by, the Baker pounced on her.

"Oh, Providence!" Jack gasped breathlessly on noticing his cow. "My Milky-White!" he exclaimed, and ran up to the cow and kissed her nose.

"Look what this hen has laid," squealed the Baker, finding a golden egg in his hand.

"You see, I promised you more than the five gold pieces I gave you," declared Jack, beaming.

"N-now, I never said I would sell—" the Baker stuttered, hoping an excuse would come to him.

"But you took the five gold pieces!" cried the boy.

"You took five gold pieces?" repeated the Wife in disbelief.

"I didn't *take*—"

"You said I could have my cow," shouted Jack, growing upset.

"Now, I never said you *could*," replied the Baker, desperately searching for a way out. "I said you *might*."

"You would take money before a child?" gasped the Wife, horrified.

Before the Baker could respond, a heavy thump jolted the ground. Milky-White had suddenly dropped dead.

WITH TWO MIDNIGHTS GONE, the exhausted and bedraggled Baker and his wife buried Milky-White and sent the sad Jack home. They pondered the new day's tasks. The Baker assigned the appropriation of a new cow to his wife.

"And what do you propose I use to purchase this cow?" she asked sharply.

Her husband dug around in his pockets and found nothing but a few lint balls and the remaining bean.

"Here," he said. "Tell them it's magic."

"No person with a brain larger than this is going to exchange a cow for a bean," she said, looking at the bean with disdain.

"Then steal it," said the Baker impatiently.

"Steal it? Just two days ago you were accusing *me* of exercising deceit in securing the cow."

"Then don't steal it and resign yourself to a childless life."

The bickering continued until the Baker agreed to procure a new cow while his wife would seek out the golden slipper, whereupon they parted company.

Unfortunately for Rapunzel, the Witch discovered her affections for the Prince before he could spirit her away. This time, however, the Witch would take no pleasure in meting out punishment, for Rapunzel was the sole occupant of the old crone's shriveled heart.

Once inside the tower, the Witch unsheathed her scissors, the sight of which caused Rapunzel to shriek in horror. "What did I say?" scolded the Witch. "Children must listen. What were you not to do? Children must see. And learn."

Instead of answering, Rapunzel could only sob uncontrollably.

The hag twitched with rage, grabbing the girl's hair. "Why could you not obey? What would you have me be? Handsome like a prince?" Suddenly the Witch's harsh features softened a bit. "Ah, but I am old, I am ugly. I embarrass you."

"No," whimpered the girl.

"You are ashamed of me!"

"It was lonely atop this tower," wailed Rapunzel.

"I was not company enough?"

"I am no longer a child," Rapunzel asserted. "I wish to see the world."

For a long moment the Witch gazed at her adopted daughter, recognizing her again as the innocent to whom she had devoted herself. "Don't you know what's out there in the world? Stay with me," she implored as she stroked the girl's hair. "Princes wait there in the world, it's true—princes, yes, but wolves and humans, too. Stay at home. I am home.

"Who out there could love you more than I? What out there that I cannot supply? Stay with me, the world is dark and wild. Stay a child while you can be a child. With me."

Rapunzel's only response was her continued sobbing; never once did she cast her eyes toward the old one. The Witch knew that an attempt to restore the past would be futile. She could imprison the girl's body but never again her heart.

"Why didn't you tell me you had a visitor?" she snarled. "I will not share you, but I *will* show you a world you've never seen!" With a raging fury, the Witch raised her scissors and tore into Rapunzel's glorious mane of hair. Amid screams and cries for mercy, the Witch chopped away at the golden locks until there was nothing left on Rapunzel's head but stubble. The enchantress then snapped her fingers, instantly exiling the grief-stricken girl to a remote desert.

Later, when the Prince tried to scale the walls of the tower, he was surprised by the Witch, who used Rapunzel's shorn locks to lure him up. Cackling evilly, she released her hold on the hair, and the Prince fell into a patch of thorns. His eyes were pierced on impact, and he was blinded.

IN THE MEANTIME, the Baker, who was wondering how he could replace Milky-White, was surprised by a familiar voice.

"When is a white cow not a white cow?"

As the Mysterious Old Man came out from behind the bushes, the Baker said irritably to him, "Your questions make no sense. Leave me alone!" But as he turned to leave, the Old Man surprised him by returning the sack of gold pieces, which he told the Baker to use to purchase a cow.

While this was going on, Jack, who was wending his way home with his new pet hen, came upon Little Red Ridinghood, who was looking quite fashionable in her new wolf cape.

"What a beautiful fur cape!" exclaimed Jack.

"Stay away from my cape," warned the little girl, whirling on him suddenly with a knife.

"I don't want it. I was just admiring it," said Jack, retreating.

"Oh," said the girl, mollified. "Well, my Granny made it from a wolf who attacked us."

"Well, look what I have," Jack said, smirking. "A hen that lays golden eggs. I stole it from the kingdom of the Giant," he added, pointing upward. "And if you think this is something, you should see the golden harp the Giant has. It plays the most beautiful tunes without your even having to touch it."

"Of course it does," mocked Little Red Ridinghood. "Why don't you go up there right now and bring it back and show me."

"I-I could," stuttered Jack.

"You could not, Mr. Liar," she snapped, and ran away, laughing.

Jack shouted after her, "I am not a liar! I'll get that harp! You'll see!"

As for Cinderella, she returned from her third visit to the festival—but wearing only one shoe. This time the Prince had deliberately smeared the palace steps with pitch, a scheme he had devised to snare his beloved as she ran from him. But Cinderella, being no fool, had pried herself free. Not wanting to be loved under false pretenses, but also not willing to completely forgo her chance to marry the Prince, she had left one slipper behind as a clue to her identity. Now, limping toward home, she was surprised by the Wife.

"Don't come any closer to me," she warned, recalling their last encounter.

"Please, just hear me out," pleaded the Baker's Wife.

"We have nothing to discuss. You have attacked me once before," Cinderella accused, backing away.

"I did not attack you, I attacked your *shoe*. I need it to have a child."

"That makes no sense," replied Cinderella.

Desperate, the Wife scrabbled around in her pocket. "Here! Here is a magic bean in exchange for your shoe."

Cinderella looked down at the bean that had been placed in her hand. "Magic bean! Nonsense!" And she threw it away.

Shouts in the distance now caught their attention. Cinderella became alarmed.

"Here, take my shoes. You'll run faster," the Wife cunningly suggested. Without further thought, the girl slipped into the woman's shoes and sped away, leaving the golden slipper in exchange.

The Baker came into the clearing leading a new cow just as the Prince's Steward came into the same clearing from another path. "I've the cow!" the Baker called out to his wife.

"And I've the slipper!" said the Wife, delighted. "We've all four!"

But as she held the shoe aloft, the Steward snatched it from her. What a trophy he now had to present to his prince!

"It's mine!" cried the Wife, struggling furiously to retrieve the shoe.

Just then a deafening crash shook the forest to its roots. All three were thrown to the ground, where they remained, stunned.

The ensuing stillness was broken when the Prince ran in. "What was that noise?"

Ever ready to assuage royalty, the Prince's Steward pronounced it to be lightning and thunder in a distant kingdom. Then he resumed his contest with the Baker's Wife for the slipper.

"Give her the slipper and all will come to a happy end," said the Mysterious Old Man, sneaking up from behind them.

"Who are you?" demanded the Steward.

"When first I appear, I seem deleterious—" began the Old Man.

"Oh, shut up!" growled the Steward with impatience.

"Do as he says," commanded the Prince. "He's obviously a spirit of some sort, and we only need one slipper. You see, I had the entire palace staircase smeared with pitch and there, when she ran down, remained the maiden's other slipper." Proudly, he held the captured footwear aloft. "Of course," he confessed, "it did create quite a mess when the other guests left."

The Steward obeyed, handing the other shoe to the elated couple. Their moment of joy, however, was abruptly cut short by approaching screams.

Into the clearing ran Jack's Mother. "There's a dead giant in my back yard!" she screeched. "I heard Jack coming down the beanstalk, calling for his ax, and when he reached the bottom he took it and began hacking down the stalk. Suddenly, with a crash, it fell, but there was no Jack. For all I know he's been crushed by the ogre." She was overcome with tears.

"Worrying will do you no good," lectured the Prince sympathetically. "If he's safe, he's safe. If he's been crushed, well then, there's nothing any of us can do about it, now is there?" No one was quite sure how to respond to this. He was, after all, the Prince.

"Doesn't anyone care that a giant has fallen from the sky?" Jack's Mother asked plaintively as the Prince and his steward withdrew.

The Baker and his wife collected their treasures to present to the Witch, who suddenly appeared before them in another smelly cloud of smoke.

"The third midnight is near," she said with a sneer. "I see a cow, I see a slipper—"

"And the cape as red as blood," piped up the Baker, who was holding his nose because of the overwhelming stench.

"And the hair as yellow as corn," added his wife.

The old sorceress looked surprised. "You mean you've all the objects?" She drew nearer for inspection. "That cow doesn't look as white as milk to me," she said suspiciously.

"Oh, she is, she is," reassured the Wife, patting the cow's rump. As she did this, a cloud of white powder rose into the air.

"This cow's been covered with flour!" screamed the Witch.

"Well, we did have a cow as white as milk, but she died," explained the Baker. "We thought you'd prefer a live cow."

"Of course I'd prefer a live cow!" screamed the Witch. "So bring me the dead cow, and I'll bring her back to life!"

"You can do that?"

"*Now!*" she screamed, hurling a lightning bolt at the Baker's feet.

The Baker and his wife raced to Milky-White's nearby grave, and with bare hands unearthed the bovine carcass, heaved it out of its not-quite-final resting place, and slowly dragged it toward the Witch.

Jack's Mother, still sobbing uncontrollably, was greatly relieved to see her son, who happened by, carrying the Giant's golden harp. "You could have been killed coming down that plant," she said, giving him a smack. But Jack simply handed her the harp and raced over to the cow.

"Out of my path!" commanded the Witch. "Earth, fire, water, and light!" she screamed, and a bolt of lightning crackled from the end of her stick and struck Milky-White's forehead. Suddenly the cow started to move and struggled to her feet.

"Milky-White!" cried Jack excitedly. "Now I have three friends: a cow, a hen, and a harp."

"Quiet!" demanded the Witch. "Feed the objects to the cow."

"What?" everyone asked in chorus.

"You heard me! Feed them to the cow!" she repeated.

The Baker did as he was told and started stuffing the red cape into the cow's mouth. Milky-White chewed slowly but steadily and then swallowed. The first chime of midnight sounded. Next, the Wife stuffed the golden slipper into the cow's mouth. Although it was difficult to chew, the cow swallowed it as the second chime of midnight sounded. Finally, the Baker gave Milky-White the yellow hair.

The Witch pulled a silver chalice from under her cloak and ordered the Baker to milk. "I'll do it," volunteered Jack. "She'll only milk for me. Squeeze, pal," he coaxed her as he knelt down and took hold of Milky-White's udders. But nothing came despite Jack's feverish milking.

The Witch took the chalice and turned it upside down. Not a drop. "Wrong ingredients," she said. "Forget about a child."

"Wait!" the Baker's Wife cried indignantly. "We followed your instructions. That cow is as white as milk, the cape as red as blood, the slipper as pure as gold, and the hair as yellow as corn. I pulled it from a maiden in a tower."

"You *what*?" howled the old hag, throwing her hands up. "I've touched that hair! Don't you understand? I cannot touch the ingredients!"

"Oh, noooo!" moaned the Baker and his wife.

Just then, the Mysterious Old Man appeared and whispered in the Baker's ear, "The corn, the corn!"

"What?" asked the Baker.

"The silky hair of the corn," said the Old Man. "Pull it from the ear and feed it to the cow! Quickly!"

The Baker pulled from his belt an ear of corn, which he had been carrying for purposes of comparison, and followed the Old Man's instructions.

"This had better work, old man, before the final stroke of midnight," snarled the Witch, "or your son, here, will be the last of your flesh and blood."

"Son?" asked the Baker in astonishment.

"Yes," responded the Witch matter-of-factly. "Meet your father."

"Father? Could that be you? I thought you died in a baking accident."

The Old Man hung his head. "I didn't wish to run away from you, son, but—" He was interrupted by a bloodcurdling moan from the cow. All eyes turned to her.

"She's milking!" cried Jack.

"I don't understand," said the Baker to his father.

"Not now," said the Old Man. He turned to see the Witch take the cup from under the cow's udder and swallow its contents in one mighty gulp.

As the clock struck midnight, the Witch slumped, her head dropping to her chest. She began turning ever so quickly, as if she were churning herself into butter. A cloud of pink smoke, this time like perfume, enveloped her until she was nothing but a spinning blur. As the haze dissipated, there emerged a stunning young woman of unsurpassable beauty surrounded by a heap of the Witch's old robes.

The Mysterious Old Man let out a cry and collapsed. The Baker ran to him. "Son," whispered the Old Man, "all is repaired." And he died peacefully in his son's arms as the Witch squealed with delight at her restored loveliness.

AND SO THE MYSTERIOUS OLD MAN ended the curse on his house. As for the Baker, there would be no reunion with his father, and he and his wife, bewildered, returned home. The Witch, who had been punished by her mother with age and ugliness on the night when her beans had been stolen, was now returned to her former state of youth and beauty. And Milky-White, after a night of severe indigestion, was reunited with the now wealthy Jack.

As for the Prince, he began his search for the foot to fit the golden slipper.

When he came to Cinderella's house, the Stepmother took the slipper into Florinda's room. But struggle as she might, she could not make her daughter's foot fit into the shoe. Finally, desperate for a royal son-in-law, she fetched a meat cleaver from the kitchen and sliced off the girl's big toe. Florinda swallowed the pain and joined the Prince on his horse, but as they rode off through the woods, they passed by the grave of Cinderella's mother, where they heard the ghost declare: "Look at the blood within the shoe, this one is not the bride that's true. Search for the foot that fits."

The Prince looked down at the bloodstained shoe and returned the false bride at once. He then handed the shoe to the Stepmother, who took it to Lucinda's room. Again, it would not fit, so the Stepmother pared the girl's heel down to the appropriate size. Lucinda, like her sister before her, also swallowed the pain, but as the Prince helped her onto the back of his horse, he again noticed the telltale blood trickling from the shoe. He yanked the shoe from her foot and demanded of the Stepmother, "Have you no other daughters?"

The woman replied, "No, although there is a little stunted kitchen wench which my husband's late wife left behind. But she is much too dirty. She cannot show herself."

"I insist," insisted the Prince.

And when Cinderella presented herself and tried on the slipper, it fit like a glove.

"This is the true bride!" announced the Prince, and much to the dismay of the Stepmother and Stepsisters, he took Cinderella on his horse and rode off.

As they passed her mother's grave, they heard: "No blood at all within the shoe, this is the proper bride for you, fit to attend a prince!''

As for Rapunzel, she had borne twins and was living impoverished in the desert. One day her blind prince, wandering aimlessly, heard a voice so familiar that he stumbled toward it.

When he approached, Rapunzel, overjoyed at seeing him, threw her arms around him, weeping. Two of her tears dampened his eyes, and their touch restored his vision.

At that moment, however, the Witch, newly transformed, came upon them.

''I was going to come fetch you as soon as you learned your lesson,'' she exclaimed brightly to Rapunzel.

''Mother?'' Rapunzel asked, recognizing the voice but not the face.

''Yes! This is who I truly am! Come with me, child,'' said the Witch, holding out her hand. ''We can be happy as we once were.''

''She will not go with you,'' asserted the Prince, pulling Rapunzel back to his side.

An argument ensued, but much as the Witch pleaded, Rapunzel resolved to stay with her Prince.

''You give me no choice,'' the Witch said ominously. The couple embraced each other as the Witch wound herself up to cast her ultimate spell upon them. *''Earth, air, water, and light! Spin your circle, make it night!''* she chanted, jabbing her stick toward them.

But nothing happened, for, as is often the way in these tales, in exchange for her youth and beauty the Witch had lost her powers. So the new family returned to the Prince's palace as the powerless Witch wandered away in disbelief.

Cinderella's wedding was attended by Lucinda and Florinda, who both wished to win favor with their stepsister and share in her good fortune. But as the wicked sisters stood outside the chapel, vengeful pigeons swooped down upon them and pecked out their eyes, punishing them for their cruelty with blindness.

Despite this unfortunate incident, it came to pass that all that had seemed wrong was now right. The kingdom was filled with joy, and those who deserved to were certain to live a long and happy life.

Or so they thought. . . .

PART II

Once upon a time, later,

in the same far-off kingdom,

lived the young princess Cinderella,

the wealthy lad Jack,

and the Baker, his wife,

and their newborn baby.

Cinderella wished more than anything, more than footmen, to sponsor a festival.

Jack wished more than anything, more than the moon, to return to his adventures in the sky.

The Baker and his wife were wishing, too. For one thing, they wished their baby wouldn't cry so much. But they also wished, more than anything, more than life, more than the moon, more than riches, that they had more room in their cottage.

The Baker's Wife wished to move, but the Baker insisted that they remain in his ancestral home, although it was with the promise that he would add on more rooms. They were arguing this point one day when suddenly a terrifying jolt shook their home. A second jolt cracked the plaster, while still another jiggled the jars from the shelves. Quickly, the Wife grabbed the baby and fled the house just as the roof came crashing down. After a long, terrible moment, the Baker, buried under rubble, stirred and began to dig himself out.

As he and his wife stood staring at their ruined house, the Witch from next door crawled over the rubble to report that her garden had also been destroyed.

"What could have done such a thing?" asked the bewildered Wife.

"An earthquake," surmised the Baker.

"No earthquake," countered the Witch. "My garden has been trampled. Those are footprints."

"But who—?" wondered the Baker's Wife.

"Anything that leaves a footprint that large is no 'who,' " retorted the Witch.

"Do you think it was a bear?" asked the Baker.

"A bear?" the Witch snorted. "Bears are sweet! Besides, you ever see a bear with forty foot feet?"

They eliminated the possibility of its being a dragon, a manticore, or a griffin, but when "giant" was mentioned, the Witch stopped pacing. "Possible—very, very possible."

"Maybe we should tell someone," suggested the Wife. "The royal family, perhaps."

"I wouldn't count on that family to snuff out a rat," the Witch cackled. "With a giant, we'll all have to go to battle. A giant's the worst! A giant has a brain. Hard to outwit a giant. A giant's just like us—only bigger! Much, much bigger. So big that we are just an expendable bug beneath its foot."

She stepped—*boom!*—on a passing cockroach—*crunch!*—to illustrate her point. She then picked the bug from the bottom of her shoe, ate it with one slurp, and returned to her home.

The Baker, deciding to ignore the advice of anyone who ate bugs, set off for the palace. First, however, he stopped by the house where Jack and his mother lived.

"Look, Milky-White," said Jack to his cow, "it's the Butcher."

"The Baker," corrected the Baker, looking annoyed.

"What can we do for you, sir?" asked Jack's Mother.

When the Baker told them of his fears, Jack's Mother said that there was nothing she or Jack could do to help and then reminded him of the time that she had reported the presence of a giant and no one had come to her aid.

Undeterred, the Baker proceeded to the palace. Although the Prince was away on business, Cinderella promised to report the news to him upon his return. After the Baker left, Cinderella was visited by her fine feathered friends.

"Oh, good friends, what news have you?"

A din of excited twittering arose as various reports from all corners of the kingdom came flying in.

"What of Mother's grave? What kind of trouble?" asked Cinderella with concern.

The birds all chirped at once, urging her to investigate.

''But a princess cannot go into the woods unescorted!''

A nightingale fluttered down and warbled a plan in Cinderella's ear.

''Good idea.'' Cinderella nodded. ''I will disguise myself as a peasant and go into the woods to investigate.''

Meanwhile, the Baker had returned to his damaged home to rejoin his wife and baby. Just at that moment, Little Red Ridinghood knocked on what was left of the door. She had come by in the hope that she could pick up some food for her Grandmother, to whose house she was relocating. The girl related how she had returned to her own house to find it destroyed and her mother gone. She believed a big wind had done the damage and thought that the safest place to head for would be her Granny's cottage.

The Baker's Wife agreed that the child should not be alone in the woods when ''big winds'' were blowing and insisted that she and her husband and child accompany her. The Baker acceded grudgingly.

Now, although Jack had promised his mother that he would stay home while she went to market, the idea of giants and adventure preyed on his young mind until he could stand it no longer. He waited until she was safely down the road, donned his boots, and dashed into the woods.

THE WOODS SEEMED EERIE, devastated. The birds no longer sang. The natural order of things was broken. Fear and uncertainty gripped the hearts of those who entered. It was a different world.

The Baker and his wife and child, with Little Red Ridinghood, moved cautiously along the now unrecognizable path. Pausing momentarily to seek out a familiar landmark, they were frightened away by the shriek of a madwoman running through the woods.

It was Rapunzel, who had lost her mind. She had attracted the maternal attention of the Witch, who now also came into the clearing.

"What are you doing here, Rapunzel?" the Witch demanded. "What's the matter?"

Rapunzel stopped dead in her tracks, turned slowly toward the Witch, and started to laugh hysterically. "Oh, nothing!" she burbled. "You just locked me in a tower without company for fourteen years, then blinded my prince and banished me to a desert where I had little to eat and, again, no company. And then I bore twins!"

"I was just trying to be a good mother," the Witch offered contritely. "Stay with me. There's a giant running about."

But there was no consoling the girl; she ran off again through the trees, while the Witch pathetically followed.

Rapunzel's Prince, puzzled by his wife's behavior, had been following her, too. During his journey, he found his brother alone in the woods.

"Good brother, why are you here?" he asked.

"I am investigating news of a giant," answered the other.

"You? Why, even Father would not do that. That is business for your steward, or less."

"Well, what brings *you* to the wood?" Cinderella's Prince asked defensively.

"My Rapunzel has run off."

"Run off?"

"She's a changed woman. She has been subject to hysterical fits of crying, moods that no soul could predict. I know not what to do." He paused. "How is Cinderella?"

"She remains well," answered his brother vaguely.

"Does she? Now, brother, I know you too well. Do tell me what you're really doing here."

Cinderella's husband looked at Rapunzel's for a searching moment, then confessed: "High in a tower, like yours was, but higher, a beauty's asleep. All round the tower a thicket of briar a hundred feet deep. Agony! No frustration more keen, when the one thing you want is a thing that you've not even seen."

Moved by his brother's words, Rapunzel's Prince admitted, "I've found a casket entirely of glass—"

His brother shrugged.

"No—it's unbreakable. Inside (don't ask it) a maiden, alas, just as unwakeable. Unmistakable agony! Is the way always barred? She has skin as white as snow."

"Did you learn her name?"

"No, there's a dwarf standing guard."

Cinderella's Prince continued with *his* problem. "If it were not for the thicket..."

"A thicket's no trick. Is it thick?"

"It's the thickest."

"The quickest is pick it apart with a stick."

"Yes," agreed Cinderella's Prince. "But even one prick—it's my thing about blood."

"Well, it's sick."

"It's no sicker than your thing with dwarves."

"*Dwarfs!*"

"Dwarfs..."

"Dwarfs are very upsetting," lamented Rapunzel's Prince.

"Agony!" cried his brother.

"Misery!" moaned the other.

But in the end they came to their senses and agreed that the best thing for now was to return to their wives.

At that moment, a scream sounded in the near distance. "Rapunzel," sighed her Prince. "I must be off." And with that, he departed in her direction.

Later that day the Baker's party had not gone far when it encountered the Steward leading Cinderella's father and stepfamily, who were all fleeing the palace, which had been set upon by the giant. The Baker's Wife wished to return immediately to the village, but the Witch, rushing down the path from that direction, said the giant had just returned to their neighborhood.

"All that's left of my garden is a sack of beans. And there's not much left of your house, either."

Suddenly the ground began to rumble. The sky darkened. Sounds of crashing and crunching grew louder as a vast shadow spread over the panic-stricken group. When the rumbling finally stopped, they fearfully raised their eyes up and up and up until somewhere way above the treetops they saw a face looking back at them.

"The giant's a *woman*!" gasped the Witch in amazement.

"WHERE IS THE LAD WHO KILLED MY HUSBAND?" boomed the Giantess.

"There is no lad here!" volunteered the Steward.

"I WANT THE LAD WHO CLIMBED THE BEANSTALK!"

"We'll get him for you, right away," answered the Witch, then cautioned, *"Don't move!"*

Little Red Ridinghood drew her knife and ran forth. "It was you who destroyed our house, not a big wind!" she yelled defiantly. "It's because of you I've no mother."

"AND WHO DESTROYED MY HOUSE?" bellowed the Giantess. "THAT BOY ASKED FOR SHELTER, AND THEN HE STOLE OUR GOLD, OUR HEN, AND OUR HARP! HE KILLED MY HUSBAND! I MUST AVENGE THE WRONGDOINGS!"

"We told you he's not here!" shouted the child.

The Giantess, who was nearsighted, remained convinced that she had found the lad. There was no consensus among the group as to which course of action to take.

"Put a spell on her," suggested the Baker's Wife to the Witch.

"I no longer have my powers. If I did, do you think I'd be standing here with the likes of you," the Witch growled. "We'll have to give her someone."

"Who?" the others asked in unison.

"The Steward," suggested the Witch slyly. "It's in his line of duty to sacrifice his life. . . ."

"Don't be ridiculous," countered the Steward, as everyone turned and looked at him. "I'm not giving up my life for anyone."

"I'M WAITING!" boomed the voice from above.

Jack's Mother, who had heard the commotion, dashed in during the argument and yelled with all the protectiveness that maternal instinct could muster, "Jack is just a boy! We had no food to eat, and he sold his beloved cow in exchange for magic beans! If anyone is to be punished, it's the man who made that exchange!"

The Baker squirmed with discomfort and tried to quiet the woman.

"HE WAS YOUR RESPONSIBILITY!" roared the Giantess. "NOW I MUST PUNISH HIM FOR HIS WRONGS!"

"We've suffered, too!" countered Jack's Mother. "Do you think it was a picnic disposing of your husband's remains?"

"DON'T GET ME ANGRY!" was the rumbled reply.

"What about *our* anger? What about *our* loss?" shouted Jack's Mother, working up a head of steam. "Who's been flouncing through our kingdom? I'll hide my son and you'll *never* find him. *Never!*"

"I'M WARNING YOU . . . !"

But Jack's Mother was out of control. "If you don't go back to the sky this instant, we'll—" Her diatribe was cut short by a blow to her head from the Steward. He had come up from behind and, in an effort to quiet her, struck her with his staff.

Jack's Mother weaved and staggered, then finally collapsed in the Baker's arms. Fighting for breath, she looked up and whispered, "Don't let them get Jack."

"We won't," reassured the Baker's Wife softly.

"Promise me you won't let him be hurt. As I stand here at death's door—" she fluttered, looking into the Baker's eyes.

"I'll do all I can," said the Baker hesitantly.

"Promise!"

"All right, I promise."

And with that, the old woman died.

"You killed her," the Baker's Wife said to the Steward.

"I was thinking of the greater good. That's my job."

Suddenly, Rapunzel ran up to the group, followed by her husband, who had been chasing her through the forest.

"IS THIS THE BOY?" thundered the nearsighted Giantess.

"No, no, this is not the boy!" yelled the Witch, restraining Rapunzel.

"He's hiding in the church steeple on the outskirts of the village," lied the Steward.

"IF HE'S NOT, I'LL RETURN TO FIND *YOU!*" warned the Giantess, moving in the direction of the village.

At which point Rapunzel, torn between her guilt over the Witch and her love for her husband, suddenly broke free of the Witch's hold, lunged across the Giantess's path, and with a final shriek threw herself under the Giantess's foot.

The others turned away, stunned by the innocent Rapunzel's ghastly end. The Witch, left standing by herself, stared after her, softly lamenting: "This is the world I meant. Couldn't you listen? Couldn't you stay content, safe behind walls, as I could not?" She sighed.

"No matter what you say, children won't listen. No matter what you know, children refuse to learn.

"Guide them along the way, still they won't listen. Children can only grow from something you love to something you lose...." Anguished, the Witch stopped her musings and returned her attention to the others.

Like rats explaining their deserting a sinking ship, the royal party announced that they were off to a hidden kingdom, but that they couldn't take everyone with them.

The Baker protested. "You'll never get there! We have to stay and find our way out of this situation together."

But his pleas fell on deaf ears, and the royal party left.

Little Red Ridinghood was angry. "I hope the Giantess steps on them all."

"You shouldn't say that," said the Baker's Wife.

"You were thinking the same thing," the Witch snapped.

"This is terrible," cried Little Red Ridinghood. "We just saw two people die."

"Since when are you so squeamish?" asked the Witch. "How many wolves have you carved up?"

"A wolf's not the same thing."

"Ask a wolf's mother," retorted the Witch. "I suggest we find that boy now and give her what she wants."

"If we give her the boy, she'll kill him, too," said Little Red Ridinghood.

"And if we don't, she'll kill half the kingdom."

"One step at a time," interjected the Baker's Wife. "Maybe if he apologizes. Makes amends."

"Yes," added the Baker. "He'll return the stolen goods."

"He's really a sweet boy at heart," continued the Wife hopefully. "She'll see that."

"You people are so blind," sneered the Witch. "It's because of that boy there's a giant in our land. While you continue *talking* about this problem, I'll find that lad and *I'll* serve him to the Giantess for lunch!" And with a great flourish of her cape, she turned and stormed away into the woods in search of Jack.

Little Red Ridinghood was shocked. "Are we going to let her give him to the Giantess?"

"No," said the Wife. "We'll find the boy first and see to it that he apologizes."

"She seemed like a reasonable giant," added the Baker.

The Baker and his wife decided that while Little Red Ridinghood stayed with the baby, they would fan out in different directions. They would count their steps from the center so as not to get lost.

ON THE WIFE'S EIGHTY-THIRD STEP, she crossed paths with Cinderella's Prince. Surprised, she politely curtsied. He acknowledged her with a nod and had begun to walk on when she timidly asked if he had seen the Giantess. When he answered no, she eagerly reported that, indeed, she had.

"You have?" asked the Prince, his curiosity piqued. "And why are you alone in the woods?"

"I came with my husband," the woman began. "We were—well, it's a long story."

"He would let you roam alone in the woods?" asked the Prince.

"No, actually, it was my choice. I'm looking for a lad."

"Your choice?" intoned the Prince, approaching her. "How brave."

"Brave?"

"Yes," he said smoothly, brushing her cheek with his forefinger. "Anything can happen in the woods. May I kiss you?" He did. She stepped back, stunned. "Any moment we could be crushed," he continued.

"Oh, uh," she stuttered, not having a lot of experience in these matters.

"Don't feel rushed," he murmured as he gently enclosed her in his dark velvet embrace.

"This is ridiculous," she thought. "What am I doing here? I'm in the wrong story." With that she pulled away and straightened herself.

"Wait a moment. We can't do this," she said. "You have a princess. And I have a—baker—"

"Of course, you're right. How foolish," he said soothingly. He drifted behind her and, gently placing his hands on her shoulders, breathed hotly in her ear. "Foolishness can happen in the woods. Once again, please."

He kissed her lightly, then assured her, "Let your hesitations be hushed. Any moment, big or small, is a moment after all. Seize the moment; skies may fall any moment." He seized her, kissing her with a greater passion than before. She lingered a second, then broke free again.

"But this is not right," she protested weakly.

"Right and wrong don't matter in the woods," rhapsodized the Prince, "only feelings. Let us meet the moment unblushed. Life is often so unpleasant, you must know that as a peasant. Best to take the moment present as a present for the moment." Between each sentence he gently touched his lips to hers until she melted in his arms. Then, tenderly, he lifted her up and silently carried her to a nearby glade.

Heading in the opposite direction, the Baker came upon the Prince's young wife, Cinderella, now disguised in the lowly rags of the scullery maid that she had once been. She was sitting on the fallen tree where her mother had been buried. She was crying.

"What's wrong, ma'am?" asked the Baker politely. "May I help you?"

"Mother's grave is destroyed," she recounted tearfully. "My wishes have just been crushed."

"Don't say that," said the Baker.

"It's true," she replied. "You wouldn't understand."

"Well, you can't stay here," he maintained, attempting to convey an air of authority. "There's a giant on the loose."

"I'm certain the Prince will see to it that the giant is rid from our land."

"There's been no sign of the Prince," retorted the Baker, mildly disgusted. "No doubt he's off seducing some young maiden."

"What?" asked the disguised Princess.

"I understand that's what princes do," the Baker explained.

"Not all princes," she replied, defensive but thoughtful.

The Baker took a closer look at the young woman. "You look just like the Princess, but dirty. You *are* the Princess!" he exclaimed, removing his hat and dropping to one knee.

"Please get up, get up," she urged. "I'm not a princess here."

When Cinderella rose to return to the palace, the Baker informed her that it had been reduced to rubble by the Giantess and that her family had departed to a hidden kingdom. He convinced her to return to the others with him.

And elsewhere in the woods, the romantic interlude between their spouses came to an end.

"I must leave you," said Cinderella's Prince to the Baker's Wife.

"Why?" she asked, bewildered.

"The giant."

"The giant," the Wife softly repeated. "I had almost forgotten. Will we find each other in the woods again?"

The Prince gazed down upon her and remembered that times like these are best cloaked in poetry. "This was just a moment in the woods," he murmured. "Our moment, shimmering and lovely and sad. Leave the moment, just be glad for the moment that we had. Every moment is of moment when you're in the woods."

He straightened himself and bowed to kiss her hand. "Now I must go off to slay a giant. That is what the next moment holds for me. I shall not forget you: how brave you are to be alone in the woods—and how alive you've made me feel." He stepped back quietly, then turned and bounded away.

The Baker's Wife sat in a daze and mumbled to herself, trying to come to terms with what had just happened.

"Wake up! Stop dreaming!" she told herself, wrestling with her resurgent conscience. "It must have been the effect of the woods. What is it about these woods?"

She stood up and started walking resolutely back to the life she had momentarily left behind, back to her child, back to her husband. "After all," she told herself, "there are vows, there are ties, there are needs, there are standards, there are shouldn'ts and shoulds.

"Why not both?" she thought, pausing to pin up her hair again. "Must it all be either less or more, either plain or grand? Is it always 'or'? Is it never 'and'? That's what woods are for," she thought to herself with a shrug. "For those moments in the woods.

"Moments," she mused, smiling as she resumed walking. "Oh, if life were made of moments—even now and then a bad one. But if life were only moments, then you'd never know you had one.

"Let the moment go. Don't forget it for a moment, though. Just remembering you've had an 'and' when you're back to 'or' makes the 'or' mean more than it did before.

"Now I understand," she said with a look of contentment on her face. "And it's time to leave the woods."

So, coming to peace with herself, the Baker's Wife made her way back toward the group. Unfortunately, no sooner had she begun to retrace her steps than the ominous pounding of footsteps once again announced the terrifying Giantess's approach. The entire forest shook in increasingly violent unison. As trees crashed and the sky darkened, the Wife scurried about in panic, with no clear direction.

AFTER A SHORT TIME, the Baker began to wonder why his wife had not returned. He didn't have to wait long to hear the sad truth.

"Look who I found," screeched the Witch triumphantly as she hauled a captive Jack before the Baker, Cinderella, and Little Red Ridinghood. Rather than congratulate her, they rushed to Jack's defense, and as they did so, the Baker noticed his wife's scarf in the lad's hands.

Pulling the scarf from the lad, he demanded, "Where is my wife?"

"She's dead," responded the Witch, who told him how she had come upon Jack weeping over her grave.

"She was felled by a tree," said Jack sadly. "I buried her in a footprint."

The Baker, in shock and despair, lashed out in anger at Jack, "It's because of you there's a giant in our midst and my wife is dead!"

"But it isn't my fault," responded Jack. "I was given those beans. You persuaded me to trade away my cow for beans. And without those beans, there'd have been no stalk to get up to the giants in the first place!"

"Wait a minute," replied the Baker. "Magic beans for a cow so old that you had to tell a lie to sell it, which you told. Were they worthless beans? Were they oversold? Oh, and tell us who persuaded you to steal that gold!"

Little Red Ridinghood pointed her finger at Jack and accused him, "See, it's *your* fault."

Jack pointed at the Baker in turn. "Wait a minute. But I only stole the gold to get my cow back from *you*."

Little Red Ridinghood turned on the Baker. "So it's *your* fault!"

"No, it isn't," the Baker responded. "I'd have kept those beans, but our house was cursed." He pointed to the Witch. "She made us get a cow to get the curse reversed!"

The Witch would have none of that. "It's your father's fault that the curse got placed and the place got cursed in the first place!"

"Oh, then it's *his* fault," said Little Red Ridinghood.

Jack interrupted. "Wait a minute, though. I chopped down the beanstalk, right? That's clear. But without any beanstalk, then what's queer is how did the second giant get down here in the first place—second place?"

The others thought about this for a moment.

"Well," Jack continued, "who had the other bean?" He turned to the Baker. "You pocketed the other bean."

Little Red Ridinghood started to say to the Baker, "So it's *your*—"

"No, it isn't!" the Baker interrupted. " 'Cause I gave it to my wife!"

"So it's *her*—"

"No, it isn't," he responded, turning to Cinderella. "She exchanged that bean to obtain *your* shoe, so the one who knows what happened to the bean is you!"

Cinderella backed away. "You mean that old bean—that your wife—? Oh, dear—but I never knew, and so I threw—Well, don't look here!" And she lashed out at Jack in turn. "Well, if you hadn't gone back up again . . . "

"We were needy."

"You were greedy. Did you need that hen?"

"But I got it for my mother!" he cried.

"So it's *her* fault, then," observed Little Red Ridinghood.

"Yes, and what about the harp in the third place?" added Cinderella.

Jack pointed at Little Red Ridinghood. "*She* went and dared me to."

"I dared you to?" responded Little Red Ridinghood indignantly.

"You *dared* me to. You said that I was scared!"

Cinderella looked accusingly at Little Red Ridinghood. "If you hadn't dared him to—!"

The Baker looked round on Jack. "And if you had left the harp alone, we wouldn't be in trouble in the first place—!"

"Well, if you hadn't thrown away the bean in the first place—!" retorted Little Red Ridinghood to Cinderella.

"Well, if she hadn't raised them in the first place—!" said Cinderella angrily, pointing to the Witch. Jack echoed this accusation, then the Baker, then Little Red Ridinghood. Soon they were all furiously confronting the Witch, shouting, "It's *your* fault!"

"*Shhhhhhhhh!*" The Witch wheeled around and stopped them in their tracks with her malicious glare. They all fell silent as she spoke in a low, menacing voice: "It's the last midnight, it's the last wish. It's the last midnight, soon it will be *boom! squish!*" She pointed at her accusers and laughed sarcastically.

"Told a little lie, stole a little gold, broke a little vow, did you?

"Had to get your prince, had to get your cow, had to get your wish, doesn't matter how—anyway, it doesn't matter now. . . .

"Of course, what really matters is the blame, somebody to blame. So blame me if that's what you enjoy, just give me the boy—" She suddenly lunged for Jack, but the others blocked her way.

"No," she sneered, stepping away. "You're so nice. You're not good. You're not bad. You're just nice. I'm not good. I'm not nice. I'm just right. I'm the Witch. You're the world.

"I'm the hitch, I'm what no one believes. I'm the Witch. You're all liars and thieves. . . .

"Here, you want some beans? Have some more," she said, hurling a handful at them. As they scrambled to retrieve them, she continued, "Beans were made for making you rich. Plant them and they soar—listen to the roar, giants by the score! Oh, well, you can blame another witch. . . ."

And, despairing that she had ever wished to be a part of this world and its rules, she called out to her mother in the ether, beseeching her to deliver her from these people, even if it meant punishment with the deformities she had had before. With that, the ground beneath her broke open and she sank into it and disappeared, never to be seen again.

The group sat in silence, contrite. Then the Baker, disgusted with the lot of them, himself most of all, turned to leave.

Jack asked where he was going.

"Away from all of this."

"But you said we had to find our way out of this together," Little Red Ridinghood reminded him.

"It doesn't matter whether we are together or apart," the Baker replied. "My wife was the one who really helped. I depended upon her for everything."

Cinderella, holding his baby, asked, "You would leave your child?"

"My child will be happier in the arms of a princess," he replied sadly, and trudged away.

But he hadn't gone far before he was surprised by a vision of his father sitting on a log.

"I thought you were dead," said the shocked Baker.

"Not completely. Are we ever?" responded the Old Man.

"As far as I'm concerned, you are," the Baker continued. "It's because of you all of this happened."

"I strayed into that garden to give your mother a gift," the Old Man explained. "Haven't you ever wanted to give someone something they didn't have? How was I to know? And when she died, I felt useless. I ran from my guilt. Now aren't you doing the same thing?"

"No more questions," the Baker responded wearily. "Please. No more tests. No more curses you can't undo, left by fathers you never knew. No more quests. No more feelings. Time to shut the door. Just"—he sat down despondently on a tree stump—"no more."

The Old Man came over to him and spoke gently: "Running away— let's do it, free from the ties that bind. No more despair or burdens to bear out there in the yonder. Running away—go to it. Where did you have in mind? Have to take care: Unless there's a 'where,' you'll only be wandering blind. Just more questions, different kind. Where are we to go? Where are we ever to go?

"Running away—we'll do it. Why sit around, resigned? Trouble is, son, the farther you run, the more you feel undefined for what you have left undone, and more, what you've left behind."

He sighed. "We disappoint, we leave a mess, we die but we don't. . . ."

To which the Baker replied, "We disappoint, in turn, I guess. Forget, though, we won't...."

They looked at each other with love and understanding. "Like father, like son," they said together.

And the Old Man was gone as quickly as he had appeared.

The Baker dwelt on these words for a while, then turned around and headed back to the group.

"I knew you wouldn't give up," said Cinderella, seeing him return.

"Give me my son," he said quietly, picking up the baby. There was a momentary cheerfulness in being reunited, but soon they all fell silent, contemplating their destinies.

"Now what are we to do?" asked Cinderella. As they sat searching for a solution, the little birds fluttered down to join them. "Oh, good friends," said Cinderella, "I need your help now more than ever. We must find a way to fell the Giantess. How can you help?" She listened attentively as they chirped out all manner of plans and strategies. Then she thanked the birds, who flew off as Little Red Ridinghood stared in awe.

"You can talk to birds?" she asked.

"The birds will help," said the Princess excitedly.

The plan was clever. When the Giantess returned, she would be lured to a place where the ground would be smeared with pitch. There the birds would peck out her eyes till she was blind. Then, while she staggered about, Jack and the Baker would deliver fatal blows from up in a nearby tree.

They were all excited. The Baker, Jack, and Little Red Ridinghood headed off for Granny's house, where there was a good supply of pitch. Cinderella stayed behind with the baby.

PRESENTLY CINDERELLA'S PRINCE, still in pursuit of the giant, bounded into the clearing and strode past his wife, not recognizing her.

"Hello," he said in passing.

"The Giantess went in that direction," said Cinderella, pointing the opposite way. Her voice took him by surprise.

"My darling," he exclaimed, turning to her. "I didn't recognize you. What are you doing in those old clothes? And with a child? You must go back to the palace at once. There's a giant on the loose."

"The Giantess has been to the palace," she noted.

"No! Are you all right?"

She nodded diffidently and turned away from him.

"My love, why are you being so cold?" he asked.

"Maybe because I'm not your only love. Am I?"

The question caught him off guard. He paused and looked down for a long moment. Finally, he stared her straight in the eye and said, "I love you. But, yes, it's true."

"Why, if you love me, would you have strayed?"

The Prince cleared his throat and ran his hand nervously through his hair. "I thought that if you were mine that I would never wish for more. And part of me is as content and as happy as I've ever been. But there remains a part of me that continually needs more."

"I have, on occasion, wanted more," she responded. "But that doesn't mean I went in search of it. If this is how you behave as a prince, what kind of king will you be?"

"I was raised to be charming, not sincere," stated the Prince. "I didn't ask to be born a king, and I am not perfect. I am only human."

"I think you should go," she said, after a pause.

"Leave? But I *do* love you," he protested.

"Consider that I've been lost. A victim of the giant."

"Is that what you really wish?" the Prince asked sadly.

"My father's house was a nightmare. Your house was a dream. Now I want something in between. Please go."

He began to walk away, then stopped. "I shall always love the maiden who ran away."

"And I the faraway prince," she reflected.

As soon as he was gone, Cinderella turned her attention to the baby, who had awakened and was in need of comfort. She rocked him gently in her arms and began to hum a lullaby.

It was not long before Little Red Ridinghood returned to report that the Baker and Jack had almost finished spreading the pitch where they would ambush the Giantess.

"I'm glad you're back here to help me," Cinderella told the child. But the little girl was in need of consolation herself. She sat down next to the Princess and started to sob.

"What's wrong?" asked Cinderella.

"My Granny's gone," sobbed the child.

"Oh, no. I'm so sorry," said Cinderella. She moved closer and put her arm around the weeping girl.

"I think Granny and my mother would be upset with me."

"Why?" asked Cinderella.

"They always said to make them proud. And here I am about to kill somebody."

"Not just somebody," said Cinderella. "A giant who has been doing harm."

"But she's a person," replied the child. "Aren't we to show forgiveness? Mother would be very unhappy with these circumstances."

"Mother cannot guide you," sang Cinderella softly. "Now you're on your own. Only me beside you. Still, you're not alone. No one is alone, truly.

"Sometimes people leave you, halfway through the wood. Others may deceive you. You decide what's good. You decide alone. But no one is alone."

Nearby, Jack and the Baker had settled themselves in a treetop.

"Wait till my mother hears I've slain the Giantess," Jack said excitedly.

"Jack," said the Baker hesitantly, "your mother is dead."

The boy was stunned. "Dead? Was she killed by the Giantess?"

The Baker shook his head sadly. He recounted how Jack's Mother had been arguing with the Giantess in an effort to protect him when the Prince's Steward struck a deadly blow. "To keep her from further provoking the Giantess," asserted the Baker.

"That steward will pay for this," cried the boy. "After we slay the Giantess, I will slay him!"

"You'll do nothing of the kind!"

"But he shouldn't have killed my mother. Right?"

"I guess not," mumbled the Baker.

"Then he must die."

"Well, no," the Baker said firmly.

"Why not?"

"Because that would be wrong," the Baker stated.

"What he did was wrong," said Jack. "He should be punished."

"He will," replied the Baker, "somehow."

"How?"

"I don't know," the Baker answered, now somewhat irritated. "Stop asking me questions I can't answer."

"I'm going to kill him!"

"Then kill him," said the Baker, without thinking. "No, don't kill him!"

The Baker wanted to give Jack the right advice, but never having had a fatherly role model, it wasn't easy to find the right words. "Wrong things, right things," he said, casting about for a beginning. "Who can say what's true? Do things, fight things. You decide. But you are not alone. No one is alone, believe me."

Cinderella joined him, addressing Little Red Ridinghood. "You move just a finger, say the slightest word, something's bound to linger, be heard. Careful, no one acts alone.

"Fathers, mothers, people make mistakes, holding to their own, thinking they're alone. Just remember: Someone is on your side, someone else is not. While we're seeing our side, maybe we forgot: They are not alone.

"Things will come out right now, we can make it so. . . ."

They were cut short by the reverberation of the Giantess's approaching footsteps. They braced themselves for the battle.

"Here she comes," said Little Red Ridinghood to Cinderella nervously.

"Here she comes," said the Baker to Jack.

"Remember, don't let her know our plan," coached Cinderella.

As the Giantess lumbered toward them, her dark shadow eclipsed all before it. Her jolting footstomps came to a halt in front of Cinderella and the child.

"WHERE IS THE BOY?" bellowed the Giantess.

"We don't know!" yelled Little Red Ridinghood.

"Yes, we do," contradicted Cinderella, according to plan. "We can't go on hiding him any longer. He must pay the price of his wrong-doings."

"QUICK, TELL ME WHERE HE IS!" the Giantess demanded.

"See that tree over there where the birds are clustered? Jack is in that tree, hiding."

"THANK YOU," boomed the Giantess. "NOW JUSTICE WILL BE SERVED AND I SHALL LEAVE YOUR KINGDOM."

The Giantess went in the direction Cinderella had indicated. When she reached the appointed spot, the birds flew as one, flustering the Giantess from all sides, and began jabbing and attacking, zeroing in on her eyes. Stuck to the ground by the pitch, she struggled violently, her screams of pain and rage echoing through the forest. She wove back and forth in frustration, grabbing hold of the tree.

This was the moment the Baker and Jack had waited for. Charged with fear and excitement, they brought down their clubs again and again on her skull.

At last the Giantess hit the earth, only inches from where Cinderella and Little Red Ridinghood stood, with a tremendous thud. Jack and the Baker scrambled out of the tree and joined them.

Together, the four of them crept forward and stared silently at the enormous corpse, not quite believing what they had done. They were both proud of their accomplishment and sad for everything that had happened.

"Now we can all return home," said the Baker. "And let us hope there will be no more killing." Everyone agreed.

"But where am I to go?" Jack asked. "I have no one to take care of me."

"You'll have to take care of yourself now, Jack," said the Baker. "It's time."

"No, it's not," chirped Little Red Ridinghood. "I'll take care of him."

"You will?" asked the lad, surprised.

"Yes, I'll be your mother now."

"I don't want a mother," said Jack. "I want a friend. And a pet."

"Of course, we have nowhere to go, so we'll move in with you," Little Red Ridinghood said, turning toward the Baker.

"Oh, no," he protested. "My house is in ruins, and there's . . ."

"It'll be fun," said the girl.

"But there is hardly room for—" He stopped himself in the midst of his selfish reasons and looked at them. "Of course you can come with us."

Jack ran to Cinderella. "And you shall join us, too."

"Yes," the Baker affirmed.

Not wanting to impose, Cinderella hesitated. But after a moment she replied: "I'll gladly help you with your house. There are times when I actually enjoy cleaning."

The moment turned melancholy. "How proud my wife would be of us," the Baker murmured wistfully, retrieving his baby from Cinderella. "And how sad it is that my son will never know her." He sighed. "How can I go about being a father with no one to mother my child?"

As he said these words, a vision of his wife appeared and spoke: "Tell him the story of how it all happened. Be father and mother— you'll know what to do."

"How?" he asked.

"Sometimes people leave you, halfway through the wood. Do not let it grieve you, no one leaves for good. You are not alone. No one is alone.

"Hold him to the light now, let him see the glow. Things will be all right now. Tell him what you know. . . ." As the Wife's words faded, so too did her apparition.

The baby began to cry, and the Baker sat down and rocked him a bit as the others gathered round. He cleared his throat and began a story.

"Once upon a time, in a far-off kingdom,

there lived a fair young maiden, a sad young lad,

and a childless baker with his wife. . . ."

Published by Crown Publishers, Inc., 225 Park Avenue South,
New York, New York 10003, and simultaneously in Canada by the
Canadian MANDA Group

CROWN is a trademark of Crown Publishers, Inc.

Manufactured in Japan

Library of Congress Cataloging-in-Publication Data

Talbott. Hudson.
Into the woods / Stephen Sondheim. James Lapine:
Adapted and illustrated by Hudson Talbott.
p. cm.
Summary: A book made ''after the fact'' from the greatly popular
1987 Broadway musical of the same name, which weaves characters
from several classic fairy tales into a parable about the joys
and sorrows of adulthood.
[1. Fairy tales.]   I. Sondheim, Stephen.   II. Lapine, James.
III. Sondheim. Stephen. Into the woods.   IV. Title.
PZ8.T148In 1988   88-16985
[Fic]—dc19   CIP
ISBN 0-517-57077-7   AC

10 9 8 7 6 5 4 3 2 1
First Edition